Echoes of the Phoenix Twilight

Eternal Grind Book III

Joel Poe

Joel Poe

Echoes of the Phoenix Twilight

Joel Poe

Aelloria

Echoes of the Phoenix Twilight

All rights reserved. No portion of this book may be reproduced, stored in a retrieval system, or transmitted in any form or by any means--electronic, mechanical, photocopy, recording, scanning, or other--except for brief quotations in critical reviews or articles, without the prior written permission of the author.

This book is copyright protected and registered by the United States Copyright Office

Library of Congress.

Publishers note: This is a work of fiction. Names, characters, places, and incidents are either products of the author's imagination or used fictitiously. All characters are fictional, and any similarity to people living or dead is purely coincidental.

Copyright © 2023 Joel Poe

All rights reserved.

www.joelpoe.com

CONTENTS

ECHOES OF THE PHOENIX TWILIGHT 1

CONTENTS 6

CHAPTER 1: HEART OF THE DRAGON 8

CHAPTER 2: A MOMENT'S RESPITE 15

CHAPTER 3: THE GROWING FLAME 24

CHAPTER 4: DECISION AT DAWN 33

CHAPTER 5: SHADOWS AND ECHOES 37

CHAPTER 6: THE BATTLE OF THE SHADOWING WOODS 42

CHAPTER 7: FAREWELL TO THE FALLEN 47

CHAPTER 8: THE RUINS OF ORMADROS 55

CHAPTER 9: THE OATH 60

CHAPTER 10: AN OMINOUS SYMPHONY IN SHADOWS 66

CHAPTER 11: THE VEILED PATH 77

CHAPTER 12: FROM SHADOWS TO CINDERS. 83

CHAPTER 13: STAND AGAINST

DARKNESS 95

CHAPTER 14: THE ARCANE CONSERVATORY 108

CHAPTER 15: THE FIRST LESSON 121

CHAPTER 16: TIDINGS OF DOOM 134

CHAPTER 17: THE UNEXPECTED ONSLAUGHT 141

CHAPTER 18: THE BATTLE WITHIN 162

CHAPTER 19: THE ETERNAL FLAME 168

CHAPTER 20: THE GREAT ARCHMAGE . 178

CHAPTER 21: AN UNFAMILIAR PLACE .. 183

EPILOGUE 196

Chapter 1: Heart of the Dragon

Malazar, the undead necromancer, stood over the lifeless body of the White Dragon, Oracle of the Wind Heaven's Peak. Her massive form lay still, a grotesque scene of violence and raw power. The finality of death was displayed in full glory, even for an ancient god.

"So much for an ancient god," Malazar sneered, his words echoing in the vast emptiness of the mountain peak, disturbing the silence. "They die like all the rest. Even the gods bow before the beauty of death."

In a show of macabre disrespect, Malazar gave the mighty dragon's body a dismissive kick. A god had been brought low, an embodiment of power now reduced to a mere carcass. With an aura of triumph, Malazar squatted down and plunged his skeletal hand into the dragon's chest cavity.

The sound of tearing flesh and cracking bones echoed through the mountains. With a wicked grin, Malazar yanked out the dragon's heart, a bloodied mass pulsating weakly in his hand. Blood spurted out, splattering his robe and pooling on the snow-dusted ground.

"Now, your power will course through me," he declared, his voice ringing with anticipation. Holding up the dragon's heart, Malazar could taste the metallic tang of dragon's blood in the air. He was moments away from unparalleled strength.

He was interrupted when a high-level Harpy, one of his aerial minions, dared to question him. "My lord, is it wise to—?"

His red eyes flickered with annoyance. With a swift motion, he summoned a dark tendril of energy, pulling the Harpy towards him. He closed his skeletal hand around her neck, lifting her off the ground. The creature choked, her talons clawing helplessly at his grasp.

Without a word, Malazar broke her neck, and in a single swift motion, ripped her head from her body. Both fell to the ground in a pathetic heap.

Malazar turned to the remaining Harpies, his gaze chilling them to their very bones. "Does anyone else wish to speak?"

The Harpies immediately prostrated themselves, their voices trembling. "No, my lord Malazar."

"Good."

Returning his attention to the bloody prize in his hand, he raised the dragon's heart to his mouth. The moment the flesh touched his tongue, a rush of raw power surged through him, as the essence of the ancient dragon coursed into his undead veins. His body spasmed in response to the sudden influx of power, causing him to fall to his knees.

His heads-up display (HUD) flickered as his level shot up from 100 to an unspecified value, an increase so large that the system couldn't register it. His class morphed from 'Necromancer' to 'Harbinger of Death,' a title befitting his newfound strength.

As the power continued to surge, memories of the slain dragon invaded his mind. He saw flashes of the dragon's last conversation with Joren, the Phoenix Warrior, and his companions. He saw their faces, heard their voices, felt their determination.

He finally rose, staggering slightly from the lingering power high. His blood-red eyes turned towards the terrified Harpies.

"Rally my undead legions," he commanded, his voice resounding with the power of a fallen god. "It's time we pay a visit to our old friend."

The Harpies scrambled to carry out their master's orders, their wings beating with haste as they spread out across the mountain peaks.

Hovering above the lifeless body of the Oracle, Malazar whispered an incantation, a twisted melody that wove through the air. The dragon's corpse quivered, a tremor flowing through its massive frame. Slowly, its eyes began to glow with an unnatural light.

With a chilling roar that echoed throughout the heavens, the Oracle's body came to life once more. Her wings unfurled, shimmering with the ethereal essence of the wind. But now, her once radiant scales were tainted, a sickly shade of black.

"This is your fate, Oracle," Malazar hissed, his voice dripping with sinister satisfaction.

"To be forever bound to my will…"

Chapter 2: A Moment's Respite

Joren, the Phoenix Warrior, sat alone on the outskirts of their makeshift camp, lost in the flickering shadows cast by the crackling fire. His companions, weary from their journey, huddled together in the comfort of the firelight, their voices softened to hushed whispers. The vibrant cacophony of the forest encased their campsite, a symphony of nocturnal creatures voicing their presence in the secluded canopy.

A soft rustle announced Lyra's approach. The rogue moved with the grace of a cat, soundless in the noisy world around them. Her blonde hair shimmered in the soft glow of the fire, and her blue eyes held a certain depth that was often masked behind her banterous facade.

She held out a wooden bowl, steam curling off its surface and dissipating into the cool night air. "Soup?" she offered, her voice a soothing whisper.

Joren's gaze remained on the distant trees, his thoughts far away from the warmth of their camp. "I'm not hungry," he replied, his voice devoid of its usual gruffness.

"You need to eat, Joren," Lyra insisted, her voice firm yet gentle. After a moment's hesitation, he took the bowl from her, the warmth seeping into his cold hands. He scooped up a spoonful, paused, and then took a reluctant sip.

A grimace immediately contorted his features. He turned to Lyra with a raised eyebrow, his expression a silent question. Lyra's laughter rang out, a merry sound amidst the silent forest.

"Anwar cooked, didn't he?" Joren asked, setting the bowl down. He couldn't help the slight twitch of his lips.

Lyra nodded, her laughter subsiding to a smile. "Yup."

"Figured."

Joren's gaze returned to the trees, the silent sentinels of the forest. He seemed to be looking at something beyond the visible, his thoughts consumed by an unspoken worry.

Lyra's hand gently covered his, a soft touch that cut through his distant thoughts. "Hey," she began softly. "You know I'm by your side no matter what happens, don't you? We all are."

He looked at her then, his dark eyes meeting hers in the flickering firelight. His hand closed over hers, a warm squeeze of reassurance. "I know," he responded, his voice barely a whisper.

Their faces were inches apart, their gazes locked in an intimate dance. Lyra moved closer, her eyes half-closed, her breath a gentle brush against his skin. But at the last moment, Joren pulled away, a silent refusal echoing between them. He picked up the bowl and handed it back to Lyra.

"Go tell Anwar it tastes great," he told her. "But I'm not hungry right now."

Lyra's face fell, a hint of embarrassment shadowing her eyes. "You should still try to eat," she managed, her voice carrying a faint tremor. "We have a long way ahead." She set the bowl beside Joren, then turned and left without another word.

As Lyra's footsteps receded, another set replaced them. Kolos, the young mage, appeared from the shadows, his white hair glinting in the moonlight. He leaned against a nearby tree, his blue eyes studying Joren with a mix of concern and curiosity.

"I know you like her," Kolos said, his voice cutting through the silent night. "So why do you keep pushing her away?"

Joren met his gaze, a storm of emotions swirling in his eyes. "You know better than anyone here I might not come out of this alive," he responded quietly. "I'm not going to start something with her just so she can get heartbroken. She deserves to be happy, and I'm a dead man walking."

Kolos sighed, moving to sit next to Joren. "Life is all about taking chances, Joren," he advised, his tone serious. "Yes, you may die, but so may we all. If you deny your heart's desire now, you may regret it for the rest of your life, however long or short that might be. Love isn't a weakness; it's a source of great power. Don't be scared of it."

He stood, preparing to leave, but paused and placed a hand on Joren's shoulder. "Besides, you're not going to die if I have anything to say about it. I'm the great Kolos, after all."

For a moment, laughter filled the air, a momentary relief from the looming threats and battles. "Thank you, Kolos," Joren replied, a genuine smile crossing his face.

Kolos nodded and retreated back towards the firelight, where he joined the others, Rafaela resting her head on his shoulder. Joren watched them, his heart swelling with gratitude. Despite the danger and uncertainty that lay ahead, he was grateful for these moments of respite, and the companions he had found in this world of chaos and magic.

As he sat there in silence, Joren couldn't help but wonder if Kolos was right. Maybe he was holding himself back from experiencing the full range of emotions that life had to offer. He had always been so focused on his duty as a warrior, determined to fulfill his quest no matter the cost. But perhaps there was more to life than just battle and death.

Lost in thought, Joren didn't hear the soft footsteps that approached him, nor did he feel the hand that rested on his shoulder. It was only when he heard her voice that he realized Lyra had returned.

"Joren," she said softly, her voice barely above a whisper. "I'm sorry if I overstepped earlier. I just want you to know that, no matter what happens, I care for you deeply."

Joren turned to face her, his eyes meeting hers in the dim light. He saw the sincerity in her gaze, the unspoken emotions that she was trying so hard to convey.

He reached up and cupped her cheek in his hand, a slight smile on his lips. "I know," he whispered. "And I care for you too."

Without another word, he leaned in and kissed her softly, their lips melting together in perfect harmony.

They stayed like that for what seemed like an eternity, a single moment of communion between two souls who were all too aware of the dangers that lay ahead.

It was a beautiful moment shared between them; a tender exchange of emotions that no words could ever describe. As they embraced each other tightly, Joren's fears and doubts melted away as if by magic, replaced by feelings of warmth and contentment. He held her close to him, savoring the feel of her body against his own as they shared an intimate moment together.

Chapter 3: The Growing Flame

As night fell over their makeshift camp, the soft glow of the campfire dancing across their faces, Lyra found herself nestled against Joren's sturdy chest. His heart drummed a steady rhythm, providing a comforting undercurrent to the crackling symphony of the fire.

His gaze was lost somewhere in the distance, a thousand thoughts swirling in. Noticing his detached expression, Lyra propped herself up on her elbow and peered up at him. "What's on your mind, Joren?" She asked, her voice soft and caring.

Joren let out a sigh, the warmth of his breath mingling with the crisp night air. "I can't help but think I'm endangering everyone," he confessed. "Malazar is after me... all because of the Phoenix spirit inside of me. There's no reason any of you should have to put your lives on the line."

Lyra cupped his cheek, drawing his gaze back to her. "We're all in this together, Joren," she affirmed. "You aren't forcing us into danger. We chose this path, not just for you, but for the bigger purpose. This... this is about the future of Aelloria, about protecting the innocent lives from becoming slaves to Malazar's undead legions."

A silence fell between them, punctuated only by the soft crackling of the fire. "Still," Joren muttered, his fingers absentmindedly tracing patterns on the back of her hand. "If I was able to fully harness the Phoenix's power, face Malazar head-on... none of this would be happening. But it won't speak to me, Lyra. It won't..."

"Maybe it's a test," she cut him off gently. "Maybe the Phoenix wants to see if you're worthy, if you can find your way without its guidance." She sighed, tracing her fingers through his hair. "That's why we're heading to Antonius Silverhand. If anyone can help you unlock the Phoenix's power, it's him. He has the essence of the Storm Fox. He will know what to do."

Joren remained silent for a moment, lost in the depth of Lyra's eyes. "I hope you're right," he murmured, his fingers gently lifting her chin. The world seemed to hold its breath as he pulled her in, his lips meeting hers in a soft, lingering kiss.

In one fluid motion, he shifted, positioning himself atop her. His strong arms braced against the earth, casting a protective silhouette against the flickering fire. Lyra's gaze was drawn to the rugged definition of his muscular chest and arms, the dancing firelight painting him in an otherworldly glow.

Their eyes locked again, an unspoken promise passed between them. Then she pulled him in once more, surrendering to the moment as a passionate dance began under the endless expanse of the starlit sky. The fire in their hearts mirrored the flames of the campfire, a silent testament to the growing bond between them.

Long after the rest of their group had surrendered to sleep, Lyra's heightened senses hummed with unease. The night was too quiet, too still. The feeling clung to her, a dark omen that made her heart pound. Silently, she rose, her nimble fingers dousing the dying embers of the fire.

With cat-like grace, she prowled the edges of their camp, every instinct screaming danger. She froze as the faintest rustling of leaves reached her ears, a chilling realization washing over her. An ambush.

She darted back to the camp, her whisper piercing the quiet night as she woke the rest. Kolos blinked up at her, his sleepy voice grumbling, "What is it?" But before Lyra could explain, the forest around them erupted with the chilling sounds of Malazar's undead.

Every member of the team leaped into action, their peaceful slumber shattered by the sudden onslaught. Lyra, with her rogue's agility, danced around the undead, her dual blades slicing through them with deadly precision. Kolos, the arcane mage, cast complex spells, his staff glowing with the raw energy that burst forth to decimate their foes.

Joren stepped into his Phoenix spirit, fire blossoming from his hands to scorch the undead. Rafaela, the group's healer, worked tirelessly, casting healing spells to mend wounds and bolster their HP, her staff casting a soft glow in the chaos.

Anwar, their holy Paladin, held the front line, his sword striking with righteous fury. Yet, for all their bravery and strength, they were overrun. The undead were relentless, their numbers seemingly endless.

Anwar, seeing his friends on the brink of defeat, felt a surge of courage well up within him. Bloodied and battered, he pushed to his feet, determination blazing in his eyes. His voice rang out, a clear, commanding prayer to the Light. "In the name of all that is Holy, I call upon your aid!"

A brilliant ray of holy light split the night sky, bathing the battlefield in an ethereal glow as radiant as day. The undead recoiled, the divine light searing their unholy flesh and blinding them. Some were incinerated on the spot, others retreated, their morale shattered.

Using this opportunity, Joren and the others swiftly dispatched the remaining undead, their team's morale buoyed by Anwar's display of courage. As the last of the undead fell, Anwar sagged to his knees, exhaustion setting in.

"Anwar!" Joren rushed to his side, helping him sit. "Are you okay?"

Drawing a deep breath, Anwar nodded weakly. "I'll be fine," he assured him. "But we must leave immediately. This was merely a scouting party. More will come." With those grim words hanging in the air, the group gathered their strength, readying themselves for the journey ahead.

Chapter 4: Decision at Dawn

As the final echoes of battle subsided, a sense of urgency swept over the group. Every rustle of leaves, every hoot of an owl was a potential warning of more undead, and their next course of action hung heavy in the chilly predawn air.

Lyra moved like a shadow, her nimble fingers collecting her thrown daggers from the undead bodies. Joren, still in his fiery Phoenix form, helped Rafaela tend to Anwar's wounds, his face hardened with determination.

Kolos, meanwhile, appeared lost in thought, his flying codex fluttering anxiously in front of him. With a swift gesture, he coaxed the magical tome open, and a large, holographic map of Aelloria flickered to life.

"We don't have much time," Kolos began, his tone grim. "Our best bet is to teleport to the Shadowing Woods," he traced a path on the map with a thin finger, the path seeming to blaze a trail from their current location to a dense forest.

Anwar grunted, a mixture of pain and disagreement. "The Shadowing Woods? Are you out of your mind, Kolos? Those woods are forbidden for a reason. Even Malazar's forces don't dare to tread there."

"But that's precisely why we should go there," Kolos shot back, his gaze steady. "We'd be off Malazar's radar, at least for a while. And besides," his eyes gleamed with a glint of mischief, "I have an old friend there who might help us."

Silence fell over the group as they pondered over Kolos' proposition. Rafaela, her hands still aglow with her healing magic, finally spoke up. "We're at an impasse here. But since this quest is primarily Joren's journey, I suggest he makes the decision."

All eyes turned to Joren. Lyra gave his hand a reassuring squeeze. "Whatever you decide, Joren, I'm with you," she promised, her eyes reflecting the early dawn's light.

For a moment, Joren just stared at the glowing map. Then he turned to

Anwar, his expression serious. "Do you have a better idea, Anwar?"

The paladin sighed, shaking his head, "No, I don't. But I don't like this, not one bit."

Joren nodded, acknowledging Anwar's concern. He then turned back to Kolos. "Then it's decided. The Shadowing Woods it is."

Kolos nodded, closing his codex as the map vanished. The air around them shifted as the mage started weaving his magic, preparing for the teleportation spell that would take them to the foreboding woods. As dawn broke over the horizon, their next dangerous step in their perilous journey was set.

Chapter 5: Shadows and Echoes

An incandescent burst of blue magic cocooned the group as Kolos channeled his teleportation spell. The world around them blurred and distorted, their senses momentarily thrown into disarray. When their vision cleared, they found themselves in the heart of an ancient forest. Trees with trunks as wide as castle turrets rose up, their thick canopies knitting together, dimming the sunlight to a ghostly half-light.

"The Shadowing Woods..." Kolos muttered, eyeing the surroundings with an uncharacteristic solemnity.

Lyra's hand automatically went to her daggers. Her senses were always sharper in the wilderness, and now they were singing with alerts. Something was off, something she couldn't put her finger on.

"There are eyes on us," she whispered, her voice barely audible.

Anwar, his brows furrowed in concentration, unsheathed his sword, the soft metallic rasp echoing ominously through the silent forest. The peace-loving Paladin was uneasy and that alone spoke volumes.

Their journey deeper into the forest was slow and tense, each step deliberately careful. The woods were dense, the undergrowth thicker than

Lyra's hair and the eerie silence disconcerting.

"Kolos," Joren began, his eyes never leaving the path ahead. "What happened here? This place feels... wrong."

Kolos gave a heavy sigh, his usual jovial demeanor fading. "This place, Joren, was once a haven. A thriving sanctuary of life. The Centaurs, they lived here. Not as masters, but as part of the forest itself. They cultivated the land, raised their young, worshipped the old gods in their sacred groves. They were guardians, stewards of these woods."

Joren tried to picture it. The Centaurs, strong and wise, tending to the forest, living in harmony with nature. But the scene clashed grotesquely with the reality around him. "What happened to them?" His voice trembled slightly.

Anwar, his gaze haunted, answered, "They were obliterated. Hunted to extinction. There's a reason the last Centaur haven is considered sacred ground. Only a handful of them were able to escape the slaughter, seeking refuge in far-off lands."

"Malazar...he did this?" Joren's query echoed Rafaela's unspoken thought. The healer turned to answer, her lips parting to utter the painful truth, but the forest had a different plan.

An unnatural, blood-curdling scream echoed through the dense woods, freezing them in their tracks. The eerie silence was shattered, the lingering remnants of tranquility dissipating in the horrifying resonance. The Shadowing Woods, once a sanctuary, now a monstrous labyrinth, had begun its gruesome welcome, casting a sinister spell over Joren and his friends.

Chapter 6: The Battle of the Shadowing Woods

The unsettling echo of the scream urged them onward, their adrenaline-fueled limbs slicing through the undergrowth. The group burst into a clearing, the spectacle before them casting a dark pallor over their faces. An imposing, level 83 Undertaker was wrestling with a wounded, elderly orc shaman.

Kolos reacted with lightning speed, lunging in front of the vulnerable shaman. His incantation was a whispered command, fingers weaving intricate symbols as a translucent, iridescent shield shimmered into existence. It absorbed the might of the Undertaker's monstrous sword with a sonorous ring, rippling with contained power.

"Engage!" Anwar roared, brandishing his sword as Joren flanked him, his fists aglow with the subtle flicker of Phoenix flames.

Rafaela had begun her sacred hymn of healing, her hands casting a warm, gentle light over the orc, her eyes narrowed in focus. Lyra darted ahead, swift as a shadow, her blades drawn, silent but deadly. The tension was palpable, the stakes higher than they'd ever been.

Anwar was a study of resolve, his blade clashing against the Undertaker's, each parry and thrust a dance between life and death. Joren moved in tandem, his Phoenix-infused fists searing the Undertaker's grotesque flesh with each punch, the smell of burnt decay permeating the air.

Lyra struck like a venomous snake, her twin blades expertly severing the tendons on the creature's legs. The Undertaker howled, its movements slowing, offering them a vital window of opportunity.

Kolos' voice filled the air, his arcane chains binding the beast, restricting its movements. It roared, thrashing against its bonds, but the spell held. Lyra's daggers flew, their target the creature's eyes. They hit home, burying into the rotten flesh, eliciting a guttural screech from the blinded monster.

Anwar made his move. With a battle cry, he parried the Undertaker's sword, locking it in a deadly standoff. His strength prevailed, and he wrenched the sword from the Undertaker's grasp, the weapon clattering to the forest floor.

Joren saw his opening. Fists ignited with the Fires of the Phoenix, he launched himself at the monstrosity. His strike was precise, deadly. The Phoenix's might decapitated the Undertaker, its massive figure crumpling to the ground, its grotesque head rolling away.

A sudden calm fell over the battlefield. Panting, they surveyed their fallen foe. Their HUD lit up, a surge of experience points flooding their vision. Their levels jumped from 57 to 60, the high-level adversary and the lingering Blessing of Will from the great stag boosting their ascent. Triumph coursed through them, their camaraderie deepening in the crucible of combat.

This was but the first step in their perilous journey, the Shadowing Woods harboring more terrors. They had won the battle, but the war was far from over.

Chapter 7: Farewell to the Fallen

Kolos rushed to the side of the fallen orc shaman, his heart pounding in his chest. Rafaela's eyes met his, a sorrowful shake of her head confirmed the unthinkable: they were too late. The life had faded from the orc's eyes, his spirit returned to the earth from whence it came.

Kolos sank to his knees, a tremor wracking his body as he cradled the shaman's lifeless hand in his own. Joren stood behind him, placing a gentle hand on Kolos' shoulder, offering silent support. The pain in Kolos' eyes was more profound than any wound they had seen him suffer.

The silence of the Shadowing Woods was broken by Kolos' voice, raw with emotion. "This shaman... he saved my life many years ago. He was noble, uncorrupted... he refused to bend to Malazar's will."

His gaze swept the darkened canopy overhead, the orc's humble dwelling barely visible among the dense foliage. "He chose this place as his sanctuary, a refuge from the world that had fallen to darkness. I guess... they finally found him."

Anwar, his expression somber, proposed, "Then we must give him a proper burial."

But Kolos shook his head, his voice barely above a whisper. "No, he would've wanted to be burned. He knew the risks of burial, of the possibility of being raised to join Malazar's legion. He would never want to be used that way."

Kolos' gaze drifted to Joren, his eyes pleading. Understanding dawned on Joren. He nodded, his hands flaring with Phoenix fire, the flames dancing and flickering like a living entity. He asked everyone to stand back as he bent over the orc shaman's body.

The fire engulfed the orc, casting a warm, pulsating glow over the clearing. The flames danced and writhed, turning the once formidable warrior into a bright beacon in the midst of the dark woods. There was a sense of profound peace, the spectacle a testament to a life bravely lived and a spirit set free.

As the flames consumed the body, Kolos rose to his feet, his voice breaking the stillness. "Go in peace, old friend, and join your ancestors." He said, his voice carrying the weight of the loss. The echo of his words hung in the air, an elegy for a fallen friend, a promise to carry on the fight, a vow to honor his memory. And with it came a renewed sense of purpose, a pledge to ensure the orc shaman's death was not in vain. They would continue their journey, their resolve hardened, their hearts steeled.

The lingering heat from the pyre slowly faded. Lyra's voice sliced through the ambient murmur of the forest, the sense of urgency in her tone unmistakable. "We need to move, if there was an Undertaker here...its undead swarm can't be far."

Rafaela, her gaze lingering on the smoldering remains of their fallen ally, nodded. "Lyra's right. We can't stay here."

Kolos, his back hunched and face etched with deep lines of weariness and pain, took a steadying breath before speaking. "But we must tread carefully. There are not just undead armies to be wary of. We've used a considerable amount of mana, which means the shadow dwellers will have surely been alerted to our presence."

With a stern look, he motioned for the group to follow. "Stay close, and follow my lead. I know a place where we can make camp."

Without a word, Joren fell into step behind Kolos, his eyes scanning the darkness surrounding them. "Let's get moving then."

As they moved deeper into the forest, the atmosphere grew palpably more sinister. The trees seemed to lean closer, their gnarled branches reaching out like skeletal hands, their shadows writhing and dancing in the flickering glow of their torches. The wind whispered through the foliage, carrying with it faint echoes of distant, unidentifiable sounds. The soft rustle of leaves underfoot was the only reminder of their own existence in this shadowy abyss.

"Someone's watching us," Lyra murmured, her voice barely louder than the rustling leaves. Her eyes scanned their surroundings, alert and wary. Her hand absent-mindedly rested on the hilt of her dagger, a familiar weight that offered her a shred of comfort.

"Focus on moving forward, Lyra," Kolos called back, his voice steady, yet strained. "Don't look back, we're almost there."

And so they continued, each step measured, each breath held. The forest around them hummed with an unsettling energy, a presence that made their skin prickle and hearts pound. The feeling of being watched, of being followed, clung to them like a second skin, an invisible threat lurking in the shadows. It was a test of their resolve, a stark reminder of the stakes, and they were determined not to falter.

But despite the menace that shrouded the Shadowing Woods, they pressed on, guided by the unwavering conviction that the fate of Aelloria rested in their hands.

Chapter 8: The Ruins of Ormadros

Through the undergrowth, the first hint of the ruins emerged—a fractured pillar, marbled and cracked, the remnants of a forgotten era. As they ventured deeper, the ruins of Ormadros unfurled before them, an eerie tableau of grandeur and desolation. Ornate structures half-collapsed, swallowed by the relentless embrace of nature, their stone surfaces moss-covered and ivy-entwined.

Kolos stepped ahead, his eyes sweeping over the decaying remnants of what was once the heart of Centaur civilization. "This is Ormadros," he announced, his voice echoing across the silent ruins. "The last stronghold of the Centaurs, their capital, their seat of power. Once home to their most sacred temples, now only rubble and misery remains."

His voice echoed through the silence, every syllable heavy with nostalgia and regret. The Centaur's lingering presence hung in the air like a spectral melody, their fractured souls trapped in an endless limbo. Their haunting lament, though unheard, could be felt—a chilling whisper in the breeze, a hollow echo in the silence, a sorrowful imprint on the crumbling stone.

Joren, captivated by the spectral beauty of the ruins, felt a strange sense of familiarity seep through him. He'd never stepped foot in this place, but an uncanny connection reverberated through him, resonating with a hidden memory. "I feel like...like I know this place," he confessed, his gaze fixated on the ghostly remnants of a long-lost era. "It's like a memory from a dream, faint yet persistent."

Anwar turned to face Joren, the silver moonlight highlighting the sharp contours of his face. "It's not surprising," he said, his voice deep and soothing. "The Phoenix, in all its fiery splendor, was said to visit the Centaurs here every solstice. They offered prayers and tributes in gratitude for the warmth it bestowed upon them—a warmth that kept the freezing winters at bay and blessed their crops with life."

His words hung in the air, filling the silence with tales of forgotten camaraderie and ancient reverence. Amidst the spectral ruins of Ormadros, under the watchful gaze of the moon, their journey continued—paved with remnants of the past, and leading towards an uncertain future.

The group ventured further into the ruins, their steps guided by an unknown force. As they rounded a corner, they were greeted with an unexpected sight—a hidden temple nestled away in a forgotten corner of the ruins. The temple was made of white marble, its columns and walls inscribed with faded hieroglyphs and ancient symbols. Vines crawled around its perimeter like clinging vines, their emerald tendrils caressing the stone surface with delicate grace.

As soon as they stepped through the entrance, a hush descended upon them. Unlike other parts of Ormadros, this temple was strangely intact; protected from time's relentless grasp by some mysterious force. In the center of it all was an altar—upon which lay the mummified remains of a Centaur leader. His body was wrapped in thick cloth and adorned with ornaments crafted from gold and precious stones. His mane was fashioned from braided leather and his face painted with intricate symbols.

Chapter 9: The Oath

As the cool night settled over Ormadros, the fading echo of the Centaur's lament grew quiet. Kolos, draped in his cloak of authority, declared, "We will camp here for the night. Inside one of these temples should suffice. We need shelter, somewhere to hide until the morrow."

Lyra gave a brisk nod, her agile form swiftly blending into the moon-kissed shadows. The rogue, familiar with solitude, was ever watchful, her instincts a living compass guiding her. Her purpose? To find a sanctuary amidst the ruins.

Meanwhile, Kolos, alongside Rafaela, ventured deeper into the spectral city. Their task was of paramount importance, for the nocturnal veil of the forest was a cloak for its shadow-dwelling denizens. The pair sought to set a protective barrier, their combined magic a beacon of hope amidst the desolation.

Joren, however, found himself ensnared by the mesmerizing allure of the ancient ruins. His gaze fell upon a half-destroyed statue, the craftsmanship exquisite despite the ravages of time. He gingerly traced the stone with his fingers, a silent tribute to the artisans of an age long past.

Anwar approached him, his gaze searching. His voice broke the silence, "How are you holding up?" The

Paladin's usual stoicism was replaced with evident worry, his gaze seeking answers within Joren's own.

Joren turned to face him, and in his eyes, Anwar saw a storm of uncertainty, an uncharacteristic flicker of fear. "Anwar," Joren began, his voice barely more than a whisper, "I have a favor to ask."

"Anything," Anwar assured him, his loyalty unyielding. But Joren's next words cut through the silence like a knife.

"If...if it comes to pass that Malazar threatens to possess the Eternal Flame, you must promise me...you must end my life." The request hung heavily in the air, a haunting proposition that echoed in the ruins of Ormadros.

Anwar reeled, his voice shaky with disbelief. "Are you insane? What has gotten into you?"

The Phoenix Warrior met his friend's shock with calm conviction. "It's the only way, Anwar," Joren asserted. "Even if it sets the Phoenix back by a century, it's better than giving Malazar control over the Eternal Flame. It would be the end of life as we know it. I can't...I won't let that happen."

Anwar wanted to protest, to refuse, but Joren cut him off. The Phoenix Warrior placed a hand on Anwar's shoulder, his gaze unwavering. "I know it's the right thing to do, Anwar. You're the only one I trust with this. I know you will place the greater good above our friendship."

Before Anwar could respond, his thoughts drowning in a tumultuous sea of emotions, Lyra's voice called out, her tone echoing through the ruins. "I've found a place!" Her announcement brought their grim conversation to an abrupt end, leaving the echo of Joren's request to haunt the silence of the night.

Anwar and Joren exchanged one last lingering look, their unspoken bond echoing through the ruins. With heavy hearts, they joined Lyra at the entrance of a dilapidated temple, its stone pillars trembling under the weight of forgotten prayers.

The interior of the temple revealed a grand hall, once adorned with ornate tapestries and glistening chandeliers. Now, only dust and cobwebs remained, clinging to the memories of a time long gone. Lyra and Anwar set about clearing the debris, creating a makeshift campsite.

As the crackling fire cast dancing shadows on the crumbling walls, Joren's mind was consumed with contemplation. The heavy burden of his request weighed on him, but he held onto a flicker of hope. Hope that Anwar would never have to set his hand against a friend, against him.

The group settled around the fire, their faces bathed in a warm glow as the night wind whispered through the broken windows.

Chapter 10: An Ominous Symphony in Shadows

A heavy silence cloaked the desolate expanse of Ormadros, its ancient stones echoing tales of a glorious past now buried beneath centuries of sorrow. Joren, unable to surrender to the siren song of sleep, found himself imprisoned by his own thoughts. Fears for the safety of his companions and the weight of his destiny seemed to echo off the crumbling stone walls of their sanctuary, amplifying his anxiety.

With a soft sigh that echoed eerily in the silence, Joren rose from his makeshift bedding. The stone was cold beneath his bare feet, a stark contrast to the warm bodies huddled nearby. He treaded carefully to avoid disturbing his friends, whose sleeping forms were the only other living presences in the temple.

The moon, shrouded by thick, foreboding clouds, cast an ethereal glow over the abandoned city, its silvery light streaming through the broken columns and windows of the temple. Drawn to the eerie beauty outside, Joren ventured towards one of these windows, his every sense alert. The nocturnal symphony of the forest filled his ears – a chorus of growls, distant and incoherent murmurs, the stealthy rustling of leaves, and the soft thud of unhurried footsteps.

His heart pounded in his chest as he peered through the narrow opening. The sight that met his gaze was something out of a nightmare. The once majestic streets of the Centaur capital were swarming with undead creatures, their grotesque figures a horrifying sight under the silver moonlight. Among them, he distinguished three monstrous Undertakers, their presence even more terrifying. One in particular stood out, its colossal form carrying the dangerous promise of a level 90. The horde was growing, its numbers increasing with each passing minute, and their presence spelled an impending doom.

The world seemed to hold its breath as Joren retracted from the window. His mind raced with strategies and worst-case scenarios as he made his way back to his friends. He woke them, his touch as gentle as the urgent situation allowed, his eyes carrying a silent warning.

"What is it?" Anwar muttered groggily, but a single look at Joren's face had him wide awake in an instant. Wordlessly, Joren led them to the window. A collective gasp filled the room as they witnessed the nightmare unfolding in the city below.

"We're surrounded," Rafaela breathed, her voice barely a whisper. Her hands trembled slightly, the severity of their situation sinking in.

In the face of imminent danger, Kolos remained calm. He turned towards Lyra, "You're our best chance. The Centaurs, they had a labyrinth of escape routes beneath the city. Can you find us one?"

Lyra swallowed hard, her eyes sparkled with resolve in the dim light. "I'll do my best," she whispered. And with a nod, she disappeared into the temple's darker corners, her fate intertwined with theirs.

Meanwhile, outside, the undead horde continued to grow, their terrifying chorus becoming a haunting serenade to the fallen city of Ormadros. The stakes were higher than ever.

Lyra moved with an elegant grace, her senses sharpened by years of navigating treacherous terrains and outwitting her prey. She trailed her fingertips along the ancient walls, seeking the hidden entrance to the labyrinth beneath Ormadros.

As she ventured deeper into the temple's depths, the air grew heavy with the scent of damp earth and forgotten secrets. Her eyes adjusted to the darkness, searching for any sign of the concealed passageway. And then, as if guided by an unseen force, a glimmer of light caught her attention—a sliver of moonlight filtering through a crack in the stone floor.

With a surge of hope, Lyra knelt down, feeling around the crevice until her fingers found purchase on the rough edges of a hidden hatch. With a gentle push, the entrance revealed itself, opening to a descent that disappeared into an unknown world below.

Lyra rushed back to her companions, her breath hurried but determined. "I've found it," she declared, her voice steadying the hearts of her friends. "There's a hidden escape route leading to the labyrinth beneath Ormadros. It's our best chance of getting out unseen."

Kolos, his eyes shimmering with a mix of relief and gratitude, nodded in appreciation. "Good work, Lyra. Lead the way. We must retreat and regroup."

Anwar drew his sword, its gleaming blade a promise of protection.

A sense of unity enveloped them as they descended into the underground labyrinth, their footsteps echoing through the winding tunnels. The air was cool and mysterious, the walls engraved with forgotten symbols of the ancient Centaurs.

As they hurried through the labyrinth's twists and turns, anticipation and urgency fueled their steps. Each dead-end they encountered was met with a swift redirection, guided by Lyra's unwavering instinct and the faint whispers of long-gone Centaur spirits.

Finally, they reached a hidden chamber at the heart of the labyrinth—a vast, circular room with a glimmering fountain at its center. The sound of flowing water soothed their troubled souls, a brief respite amidst the mounting peril.

The room was a testament to the Centaurs' architectural prowess, an amalgamation of intricate stonework and organic growth. A fountain nestled at the chamber's heart, its shimmering waters whispering ancient tales. Yet, the chamber's most intriguing feature was the series of ancient scriptures and riddles etched onto the floor in a radial pattern around the fountain.

Joren's eyes traced over the symbols, a frown of concentration etched onto his face. "These are old," he murmured, "older than anything I've ever seen." Anwar, with his natural affinity for ancient languages, joined him, his expression echoing Joren's bewilderment. Rafaela leaned over their shoulders.

Time seemed to slow as they struggled with the ancient scriptures. Each failed interpretation felt like a tightening noose. But amidst the rising tension, Kolos remained stoic, studying the scriptures with a tranquillity that seemed to imbue the room with a reassuring calm.

Suddenly, his eyes widened with recognition, and he drew himself up, his voice echoing through the chamber. "The answer has been here all along. Hidden in plain sight, the path to salvation lies not without, but within."

Turning to the fountain, Kolos stepped forward, his arms spread wide, and he began to chant an incantation, his deep voice harmonizing with the chamber's acoustics. The room shuddered in response, the ancient stones vibrating with power. The fountain's waters began to churn violently, casting out luminescent droplets that danced in the flickering candlelight.

As his chant reached a crescendo, the water parted, revealing a hidden passage beneath the fountain—an unexplored path that promised salvation. As the echo of Kolos' chant died out, a sense of awe filled the chamber. Their path was clear.

Chapter 11: The Veiled Path

The journey down the concealed pathway was a test of faith and resolve. As they entered the tunnel, darkness swallowed them whole, as though they had walked into the mouth of some ancient beast. Yet, as they moved further, an ethereal glow began to filter through the tunnel. It was as if the spirits of the Centaurs were guiding their path, casting a celestial light to ward off the enveloping darkness.

Their trek was not without its hazards. Rafaela, the usually nimble Empath, stumbled, falling onto the hard, stone floor. Kolos was at her side in an instant, his sturdy hands offering her a steady grip. The air between them thickened as their eyes met, the familiar spark rekindling. They stood there for a moment, locked in a silent conversation that spoke louder than any words could.

However, their moment was interrupted by Anwar's urgent reminder of their predicament. The need for their continued movement jarred them back to reality, leaving the unspoken words hanging heavy in the air.

Their journey resumed, with each of them lost in their thoughts. The journey felt like an eternity, with the only sound being their hushed breaths and the soft echo of their footfalls. But eventually, the tunnel gave way to a towering ladder that led upwards into the unknown.

Joren, always the vanguard, ascended first. His hands gripped the cold rungs of the ladder, muscles straining as he pushed open a heavy stone door. He peered cautiously into the moonlit exterior, heart pounding against his chest. His sharp eyes scanned the surroundings, but to his relief, no undead horrors lurked in the shadows. He signaled for the others to ascend, relief washing over his tense features.

One by one, they emerged from the tunnel, drawing in lungfuls of fresh night air. They were far from the infested ruins of Ormadros, deep in the forest, their path lit only by the ethereal glow of the moon and twinkling stars.

They journeyed further into the heart of the forest, the soft rustling of leaves and the distant calls of nocturnal creatures the only sounds accompanying their travel. Their relief was palpable, but they knew they were not yet safe.

Suddenly, their path was barred by an imposing figure, an entity forged from shadows and malice—a Shadow Elemental. Its monstrous form loomed over them, blotting out the moonlight and casting a chilling pall over the forest. Its malevolent energy filled the air, a tangible wave of hatred and anger.

Kolos stepped forward, his eyes burning with a fierce determination. He locked eyes with the elemental, standing firm in defiance. "You will not hinder our path, creature," he declared, his voice resounding through the forest.

The elemental roared in response, a cacophonous bellow that shook the very earth beneath their feet. The air around them crackled with anticipation, an epic confrontation looming on the horizon.

With the haunting echoes of the elemental's roar hanging in the air, they readied themselves for the battle ahead, their hearts pounding in synchrony. The confrontation with the shadow elemental was a cliff-edge they teetered upon, and they knew the following moments would tip the balance in favor of their survival—or their end.

As the elemental moved, a surge of adrenaline coursed through their veins. This was their moment of truth, the beginning of a battle that would test them. They had come too far to back down now, their resolve hardened in the face of impending danger. And with that, they charged, marking the beginning of their clash against the shadow.

Chapter 12: From Shadows to Cinders

The world seemed to slow around them as the elemental bellowed in challenge, a battle cry that echoed through the eerily silent forest. A rush of adrenaline coursed through their veins, each of them bracing for the inevitable. Their enemy, wrought of pure darkness and malice, stood in stark contrast against the moonlit forest backdrop.

Kolos, his arcane magic swirling around him in a vibrant display of power, led the charge. His mind was a flurry of strategy and spells, calculating the best course of attack against their monstrous foe. He realized quickly that their typical offensive measures had little effect on this creature. It was time for a shift in tactics.

As Rafaela channeled her healing powers, keeping them on their feet, Kolos began manipulating the elements, summoning ice and wind to aid them. The icy tendrils latched onto the shadowy beast, sapping its strength, while gusts of wind buffeted it off balance.

Meanwhile, Joren, the embodiment of the Phoenix, surged forth. His body ignited with the raw, elemental fire of his spirit, adding the third piece to their elemental assault.

Anwar, the holy paladin, stood like a beacon amidst the chaos, his full filigree armor gleaming in the ethereal moonlight. With his sword and shield ready, he took on a defensive stance, protecting his comrades from the elemental's shadowy onslaught. His holy light cast a protective aura around them, providing a haven amidst the battle.

And then there was Lyra. Nimble and lethal, she danced around the battlefield with her dual daggers, her every move laced with poison. Her agility and cunning kept the elemental off balance, drawing its attention away from the others. Her smoke bombs further added to the confusion, blurring the elemental's vision and hindering its attacks.

However, despite their relentless assault, the shadow elemental's vitality remained high. The situation looked dire until a sudden twist changed the tide.

Lyra, in her weariness, failed to dodge a shadow bolt that sent her sprawling. She crumpled against a tree, falling unconscious. A wave of fear and anger washed over Joren at the sight of his beloved lifeless on the ground.

The Phoenix warrior roared in fury, his aura igniting with an intensity they had never witnessed before. Flames engulfed his entire being as he charged towards the elemental, casting "Genesis: Dawn of the Phoenix". The burst of elemental fire seared through the shadow beast, causing it to shriek in pain as it burnt away into oblivion.

Kolos, recognizing the danger, scooped up Lyra's lifeless form and joined Anwar and Rafaela, quickly erecting an Arcane Shield to protect them from the onslaught of fire.

The surrounding area was swallowed by Joren's fire, the forest becoming a blazing inferno. The shadow beast's tormented wails faded as it succumbed to the flames, reduced to nothing but charred remains.

The inferno died down, leaving behind a scorched battlefield. Joren's flames dwindled, his form collapsing to his knees in exhaustion. But as he saw Lyra stirring awake due to Rafaela's healing magic, relief washed over him.

As the chaos of battle gave way to the tranquility of the moonlit forest, Joren made his way over to Lyra. His heart pounded in his chest, relief and worry intermingling as he gazed upon her bruised and battered form. His eyes, burning with the lingering flames of his phoenix spirit, bore into hers, seeking reassurance in their shared connection.

"Are you alright, Lyra?" he asked, his voice thick with concern. His calloused fingers cupped her face, the heat radiating from them soothing against her chilled skin.

"I'm fine, Bum," she responded with a weak chuckle, a nickname that held a world of shared memories and private jokes. His worry lines softened at the sound of her laughter, the sweetest melody to his ears.

"But...you took a heavy hit. I..." he trailed off, the guilt and fear apparent in his gaze. His arms instinctively tightened around her, as though he could shield her from all the dangers of the world.

"Joren," Lyra said, her voice gentle yet firm, "I've faced worse, you know that." She reached up, her hand brushing against his cheek in a comforting caress. "You really think you could get rid of me that easily?"

Her words, laced with teasing undertones, elicited a hearty laugh from Joren. His eyes sparkled with mirth and adoration, the tension from the battle finally dissipating. He was silent for a moment, his gaze drinking in her strength, her resilience, her unwavering spirit.

"No," he finally said, his voice a mere whisper against the gentle rustling of the leaves. "I couldn't dream of a world without you in it, Lyra."

Their laughter echoed through the quiet forest, a shared joy amidst the trials they faced. Their bond, forged in the fires of adversity, was a beacon of hope and strength, a promise of better tomorrows.

Joren leaned down, capturing Lyra's lips in a gentle kiss. It was a vow, an unspoken pledge of their intertwined destinies. And in that moment, under the moon's watchful gaze, they found solace and warmth in each other's arms, amidst the ashes of their battle.

Love was their greatest strength, and with it, they were invincible.

Their whispered words of love were cut short as Kolos, his gaze hardened, interrupted their shared tranquility. "I hate to intrude on this tender reunion," he began, his voice a mirthless echo amidst the quiet of the night, "but it seems our lovebirds have attracted quite the audience."

Anwar, always the practical one, shifted his weight, unsheathing his sword as he added, "And not a particularly lively one, nor even... particularly alive, for that matter."

Their words sent a chill down Joren's spine as he reluctantly pulled away from Lyra. Following their gazes, his heart sank at the sight that met his eyes. The undead swarm and the three monstrous Undertakers had them surrounded, their eerie stillness making the situation all the more unnerving.

The grotesque figures loomed ominously against the backdrop of the moonlit forest, their spectral eyes devoid of any emotion. The aftermath of their battle with the shadow elemental had clearly been too enticing for the undead, like moths drawn to the flame.

"What do we do now?" Joren asked, his voice barely audible above the deafening silence. His eyes, now glowing with the vibrant colors of the phoenix fire, were filled with a resolve that belied his exhaustion.

Kolos chuckled, a dark, dry sound that sent a shiver down their spines. His hands began to glow with an ethereal light, a spectacle of arcane magic that reflected his unwavering determination. "Well, the only way out, it seems," he said, a smirk playing on his lips, "is through them."

A brief moment of silence followed his words, as though the forest itself was holding its breath. Then Joren, his fists erupting into flame once more, rose to his feet. "Then let's get it done," he declared, a determined spark lighting up his eyes.

His words hung in the night, a declaration of their unyielding will. Their plight seemed to fade away amidst their collective determination, replaced by a surge of adrenaline and a renewed sense of purpose. With fire in their hearts and steel in their gazes, they prepared to face the oncoming storm, bound by the threads of shared destiny and the unspoken vows of enduring friendship.

Chapter 13: Stand Against Darkness

A heavy pall hung over the forest as Joren and his companions steadied themselves, their muscles coiled tight in anticipation. Before them lay an endless sea of decay and malice - Malazar's dreaded undead legion. Leading the charge were three hulking Undertakers, each one radiating menace. But one in particular stood out, a colossal abomination pulsing with unnatural power. Its health bar registered a staggering level 93.

Joren's jaw tightened. This foe would push them to their limits. But they had no choice except to stand and fight.

Failure here would doom all of Aelloria.

"Get ready!" he shouted, adrenaline surging through his veins. At his signal, they sprang into action, months of fighting side-by-side guiding their strategy.

Kolos struck first, his fingers nimbly tracing arcane symbols as he chanted under his breath. With a final thunderous command, spectral chains erupted from the earth, ensnaring the Undertakers' limbs and slowing their advance. They strained against their bonds, grotesque faces contorted in rage.

Anwar gave a mighty roar and charged forward, holy sword cleaving through rotten flesh and bone with righteous zeal. Rafaela followed closely, her healing aura radiating over Anwar, mending wounds and sustaining him against the tide.

With the Undertakers momentarily contained, Joren and Lyra broke off, carving a path through the seething undead masses. Joren's fists ignited with phoenix fire, scorching adversaries to ash with each strike. Lyra danced around him, her twin daggers dealing lethal blows before fading back into the shadows.

Step by deadly step, the companions pushed forward, their teamwork keeping exhaustion at bay. But the undead numbers barely thinned, a new fiend rushing to replace each fallen one.

A thunderous snap split the air as the largest Undertaker, the level 93 beast, finally shattered its spectral chains. It barrelled towards Anwar, cleaving its massive axe downwards. Anwar met the blow head on, though the force sent him crashing to one knee.

"Hold on, I'm coming!" Joren shouted, punching through the swarm to aid his friend. But the other two Undertakers had also broken free, their axes locking together to form a deadly spinning vortex that ravaged anyone nearby.

Joren and Lyra were forced back, unable to reach Anwar. Kolos hastily erected a shimmering shield around Rafaela, sweat beading his brow from the sustained mental effort. Lyra disappeared in a cloud of smoke, only to reappear behind an Undertaker, her poisoned blades seeking weak points in its armor.

The frenzied battle raged on, neither side gaining dominance. Step by agonizing step, Joren carved a path back towards Anwar, who was barely holding his ground against the level 93 beast. Its axe smashed down again and again, holy shield preventing a killing blow but draining Anwar's strength nonetheless.

With a primal roar, Joren unleashed a jet of phoenix fire, blasting the Undertaker back long enough for Anwar to regain his footing. "We end this now!" Joren yelled, hands burning bright.

Together, they launched at the abomination, their combined might slowly toppling its massive health bar. Fifty percent...thirty percent...twenty. Their victory seemed imminent.

But then disaster struck.

A stray axe swing from one of the other Undertakers slammed into Anwar, cutting through a gap in his armor. He sank to his knees, life force ebbing away.

"No!" Joren cried in anguish. Distracted, he failed to avoid the level 93's counterattack. A vile backhand sent him crashing limply against a tree, his health bar plummeting. Through bleary eyes, he watched helplessly as the Undertaker raised its axe for the finishing blow.

This was it. After everything, he had failed. As the axe began its descent, Joren braced himself for the end.

Suddenly, a blinding flash lit up the forest, accompanied by an earth-shattering thunderclap. The axe's killing arc halted mid-swing as a colossal lightning bolt smote the Undertaker with purifying wrath.

Joren's heart leapt in disbelief and awe. There, wreathed in crackling energy, stood Antonius Silverhand himself - the realm's most powerful sorcerer. His gaze burned with righteous fury.

"You shall torment this land no longer, fiend!" Antonius boomed, voice echoing through the trees. With another thunderclap, he teleported before the Undertaker, driving his crackling staff through its chest. It let loose an unearthly wail before crumbling to dust.

Antonius whirled, casting a rejuvenating aura over Joren and Anwar. "Stay strong, heroes! We shall purge this evil together!"

All around them, portals shimmered open as Antonius' allies joined the fray - three mighty Paragons and an ancient witch named Silvia. At their master's command, the Paragons slammed their staves down in unison, raw arcane energy rippling outwards to decimate the undead ranks.

Silvia cackled, wrinkled hands aglow, as she battered the remaining Undertakers with mystical bolts.

Within moments, the tide had turned completely in the companions' favor.

But their reprieve was short-lived. An unnatural darkness swept over the horizon, heralding the arrival of Malazar himself. The necromancer hovered above the battlefield, coal-black eyes ablaze with fury in a spectral projection. A holographic form.

"Just in time, as usual, Antonius," he spat. "Yet you're only delaying the inevitable!"

"I'm not afraid of you, demon!" Antonius challenged, "I have defeated you once. You would do well to remember that!"

"Is that so…?" said the Dark Lord, a tone of mockery and arrogance unmistakable. With that, he receded into the shadows, his chilling laughter echoing long after his form faded.

Antonius' expression was grave. "We haven't a moment to lose. We must return swiftly!" He motioned towards a shimmering portal already swirling open behind him. "Hurry now, all of you!"

One by one, they staggered through, Antonius entering last and sealing it shut. For now, they were safe. As the haze of battle lifted, Joren found himself standing in the heart of the magic conservatory, Antonius' sanctuary.

He swayed weakly, the ordeal finally catching up to him. Gently, Lyra wrapped an arm around him, supporting his weight. Despite everything, her touch still made his heart quicken.

"Welcome, friends," Antonius said heavily. "Here, you may rest and restore your strength. I only wish it were under better circumstances."

He turned to face them, pride and sadness both etched on his face.

They would sleep deeply that night, Antonius' wards keeping them hidden. But each of them knew when dawn came, the real fight would begin. Against darkness itself.

Yet tonight, they would share warmth and comfort, drawing strength from each other. And no matter how dire their odds, they would stand together, bonded by friendship and love. For within each of them burned hope's gentle flame, kindled by Antonius' unwavering belief.

In the quiet moments before sleep claimed Joren, he pulled Lyra a little closer. As long as they stood united, he knew Malazar's evil could never win. Light would prevail. With that silent promise cradled in his heart, Joren surrendered himself to dreams of better days ahead.

Chapter 14: The Arcane Conservatory

Awed silence hung over the companions as they took in the sweeping grandeur of the Arcane Conservatory. Located deep within the ancient forests of Sadrym, its towering spires rose up in a stunning display of magical architecture. Delicate bridges arced gracefully between buildings while gardens blooming with exotic flora adorned the courtyards.

Even Kolos, who had studied here as a boy, felt humbled by the sheer scale of this vast sanctuary of the mystic arts. Students robed in every color bustled to and fro, their laughter and lively discussions filling the air. High above, enchanted books fluttered around the library's open terraces like brightly plumed birds.

"Magnificent, isn't it?" Antonius remarked, pride evident in his voice. "Sadrym has been a refuge for magical learning since time immemorial. And now, it shall be a bastion against the dark forces that threaten our world."

As he spoke, three figures emerged from a nearby tower - Antonius' trusted Paragons, the elite mages who assisted in protecting Sadrym. Clad in iridescent blue and silver robes, they emanated wisdom and power.

"Esteemed friends," Antonius greeted warmly, "please meet our Paragons. Their mastery of the arcane arts is rivaled only by each other."

The Paragons bowed respectfully. " Antonius has told us much of your courage," One of them said, her voice rich and melodic. "You honor us with your presence, Phoenix."

Joren's eyes gleamed with barely restrained awe. "The honor is ours," he responded earnestly. "Your mystic talents are legendary across the land."

As Kolos conversed eagerly with the Paragons, Antonius turned to address the group. "Come, my friends. Make yourselves at home. These halls are well guarded - no darkness can infringe upon Sadrym."

With those reassuring words, Antonius led them towards the conservatory's living quarters. Lyra fell into step beside Joren, their fingers intertwining unconsciously. Amidst all the chaos, these small moments together were an oasis of peace.

They all went about their day. Except Kolos, who had received an urgent summons to Antonius' study.

Upon entering the arched chamber, Kolos was surprised to find not just Antonius, but also the esteemed witch Silvia Froggenstale. Antonius smiled, his eyes crinkling warmly beneath his silvery brows.

"Ah, Kolos. Thank you for coming on such short notice. Please, have a seat." He motioned to a high-backed chair before his desk. Kolos sat, back straight with nervous energy.

"I asked you here because matters are dire, and we require your insight," Antonius began solemnly. "Malazar is emboldened. He will seek to strike us here, at the heart of Sadrym. We must fortify our defenses."

He turned to Silvia, deferring to her wisdom. The aged sorceress leaned forward, her voice low and urgent. "Child, you have studied the necromancer up close. You know his powers. How can we best protect Sadrym?"

Kolos' forehead creased in thought. Choosing his words carefully, he responded. "Malazar commands vast armies, but his magic...it is like nothing I've witnessed." He shook his head gravely. "He corrupts life itself, bending it to serve his twisted will. His necromancy knows no limits. Even now he is in possession of the Deathreaver. He used it to kill the Oracle…"

Silvia and Antonius exchanged grim looks. "Just as we feared," Silvia muttered. Her eyes narrowed in thought before fixing intensely on Kolos again. "And the boy who houses the Phoenix spirit - can he aid us when Malazar comes for him?"

At the mention of Joren, Kolos sat straighter, a surge of protectiveness welling within him. "Joren is noble and true," he stated firmly. "The Phoenix's power flows strongly through him. But he has yet to fully master it." His shoulders slumped slightly as he admitted, "I fear Malazar seeks that which Joren himself does not yet understand."

A heavy silence settled following his words. The threat they faced was unlike anything in living memory. Finally, Antonius spoke, his voice kind but unswaying.

"Have faith, son. We shall unravel this mystery in time. For now, we must fortify Sadrym with every protection at our disposal." He rose, signaling the meeting's end. "I thank you for your counsel. Rest now - you have more than earned it."

Kolos wandered back to the living quarters in contemplative silence. Despite Antonius' reassuring words, uncertainty pooled in his stomach. A storm was coming; they could all feel it. And he desperately hoped they would weather it.

Meanwhile, in the conservatory's infirmary, Anwar rested fitfully as Rafaela tended to him. Her healing magic had mended the worst of his injuries, but his body remained weakened.

"You need to take it easy," Rafaela gently chided as Anwar tried sitting up. With a grumpy huff, he acquiesced, allowing her to adjust his pillows. Her fingers brushed against his shoulders, leaving pleasant warmth in their wake.

"I know I don't say it enough, but thank you, Rafaela," Anwar said gruffly. "Your gifts have saved my life many times over." To her surprise, he clasped her hand in his own calloused ones.

Rafaela felt her cheeks flush at the contact. Flustered, she slipped her hand free, busying herself with straightening his bedsheets.

"Of course, it's my duty after all," she mumbled. An awkward tension descended between them. Steeling herself, Rafaela asked, "Does it...bother you? Kolos and I?"

Understanding dawned in Anwar's eyes. He sighed deeply before responding. "I won't lie and say there's no jealousy. But I know where your heart lies, and I cannot begrudge your happiness."

His words carried no bitterness, only selfless love. Overcome by emotion, Rafaela bent down and kissed his forehead. "Thank you," she whispered thickly, then hurriedly excused herself.

Some time later, Lyra went looking for Joren and found him on a secluded balcony overlooking Sadrym's sweeping grounds. He was so lost in thought he didn't notice her approach until she slipped her arms around him.

"Quite a view, isn't it?" she murmured, resting her chin on his shoulder.

Joren leaned into her embrace, the familiar scent of her hair soothing him. "It's beautiful," he agreed. "So full of life and hope. But I can't appreciate it knowing how fragile it all is."

He exhaled heavily, the weight of responsibility never far from his mind. Lyra turned him gently to face her, cupping his cheek.

"You take too much onto yourself, my love," she chided. "We're here beside you, now and always. Don't shoulder this alone." She drew him down into a tender kiss, pouring her very heart and soul into it.

For a blissful moment, Joren let the rest of the world slip away, losing himself in Lyra's love. They stayed tangled in each other's arms as dusk fell over Sadrym, content simply to be together.

But they both knew this tranquility was fleeting. Dark storm clouds gathered just beyond the horizon, marching relentlessly closer. When they broke, it would unleash a deluge of chaos and ruin.

Yet here, cradled in love's embrace, the future did not seem so bleak. Together, they would weather the coming tempest, igniting a beacon of hope to guide others through the night.

Chapter 15: The First Lesson

Dawn's rosy fingers crept over Sadrym, bathing its sweeping buildings in warm golden light. Already students bustled about, eager to begin their mystic studies. But Joren felt only trepidation twisting his insides as he made his way to Antonius' private training grounds.

Today, his real training would begin. Antonius himself would guide Joren in mastering the Phoenix's flame, preparing him for the coming battle with Malazar. The stakes could not be higher.

Steeling himself, Joren stepped into the circular training arena carved of polished white stone. Arcane symbols ringed its periphery, thrumming with power. At its center stood Antonius, robed in shimmering silver.

"Welcome, Joren," the archmage greeted. "Are you ready to unlock your true potential?"

Joren gulped. "I'll certainly try, Master Antonius," he responded, unable to keep a nervous tremor from his voice. Antonius' presence was intimidating despite his gentle demeanor.

"Courage, my boy. I have utmost faith in you." Antonius clasped Joren's shoulder reassuringly before continuing. "As you know, I too harbor a powerful essence within me - that of the Storm Fox, Azyrion. Through harmony with her spirit, I attained my abilities."

Joren listened intently as Antonius went on. "The Phoenix's essence dwells in your soul, Joren. To unleash its power, you must open your heart and mind, surrendering your very being to become one with its fiery spirit."

He motioned upwards. "Watch."

Joren watched in awe as Antonius closed his eyes, brow furrowing in concentration. The air began to swirl, slowly at first, then with growing intensity. Antonius' hair and robes billowed wildly as he channeled Azyrion's lightning magic. With a clap of thunder, he released the pent-up energy skyward in a controlled ray.

As the winds died down, Antonius opened his eyes, serenity emanating from him. "Do you understand, Joren? You must relinquish all ego, becoming a vessel for the eternal flame."

Joren struggled not to feel overwhelmed. "I will try, Sir."

"Good. We shall begin with basic meditation. Clear your mind, focusing only on your breathing."

Joren settled cross-legged opposite Antonius, closing his eyes. He focused on the steady rhythm of each breath, willing his mind to quiet. But invasive thoughts kept bursting through - worries about his friends, his duty, the coming battle. The Phoenix's fire remained dormant, just out of reach.

After an hour of fruitless struggle, Joren opened his eyes, shame reddening his cheeks. "Forgive me. I failed to make any connection."

But Antonius merely smiled encouragingly. "It is only your first attempt, dear boy. These things take time and perseverance." He rose gracefully, motioning for Joren to do the same. "Walk with me."

They strolled along a winding path through Sadrym's sprawling training grounds. All around them, Antonius' students practiced their spells and combat forms with enthusiasm under the guidance of senior mages.

Joren spotted his companions among them. Kolos faced down a quintet of conjured dire wolves, fending them off with precise shockwaves. Nearby, Lyra engaged in an acrobatic duel against a charmed training dummy, testing her agility.

Anwar sparred against a Paragon, slowly regaining his strength. His movements were not as sharp as usual, but determination blazed in his eyes. Meanwhile, Rafaela sat serenely beneath a willow tree studying a mystic tome, sunlight dappling her through the hanging branches.

Seeing his friends safe and thriving, Joren's heart swelled with joy and pride. Sensing the shift in his emotions, Antonius gave him an approving pat on the back.

"Your true power lies not in solitude, but in unity with those you love," the archmage remarked sagely. "The Phoenix's fire burns brightest when fueled by the passion of your bonds."

Joren watched his companions, knowing Antonius spoke the truth. "They give me courage," he admitted. "I don't know if I could do this without them."

"Nor should you," Antonius said gently. "Embrace the love they kindle within you, Joren. Let it be the spark that ignites the eternal flame."

With an affectionate smile, Antonius gave him a light push. "Now go. Join them."

Joren hardly needed any convincing. Grinning, he ran off to spar with Anwar, the two falling into easy banter. Though Joren lacked the Phoenix's full power, joy suffused him, making his strikes more fluid and sure. For now, he let tomorrow's burdens slip away, savoring this sun-dappled moment with his dearest friends.

The day passed swiftly, laughter and determination mingling freely. By sunset, pleasant weariness had settled into Joren's muscles. Tomorrow, the real work would continue, but Antonius was right - he couldn't undertake it alone. Together, they were strong.

That night, Joren dreamed of fire - not destructive, but life-giving, like the first spark that brought light into darkness. For the first time, the Phoenix felt close, its warmth kindling his spirit.

When dawn broke, Joren arose, a newfound sense of purpose thrumming through him. After breaking fast with his companions, he bid them farewell and made for Antonius' training grounds once more.

The archmage was already present, perched serenely atop a flat-topped pillar. He peered down at Joren's arrival, eyes twinkling.

"Good morning, Master Antonius," Joren greeted, unable to keep eagerness from his tone.

"And to you, young Joren," Antonius replied. "I sense Azyrion's blessing in the winds today. Are you prepared to embrace the flame?"

Joren inhaled deeply, letting calm settle over him. "I am."

Antonius leapt down gracefully, robes rippling. "Let us begin." Taking Joren's shoulders, he steered him to the arena's center. "Focus inward, Joren. Breathe, surrender. Become the vessel."

With utmost care, Joren stabilized his mind, consciously relaxing each muscle. Gradually, his senses dimmed until only the pounding of his heart remained. He mentally chanted the mantra Antonius had taught him, cutting through conscious thought.

Deeper and deeper Joren drifted into a meditative trance. At first, there was only silence and darkness. Then, a glow appeared, faint but growing brighter, accompanied by a rising warmth. Joren focused wholly on it, fanning the fragile flame with his soul's breath.

Slowly, the fire spread, flowing through his veins in rivulets of liquid light. Joren's physical form seemed to fall away as he became one with the now-roaring blaze. Distantly, he felt his body lift off the ground, enveloped in a blinding inferno.

And then suddenly, he understood. This was no destructive firestorm, but life itself - the primal energy that burned in the heart of the cosmos. Time and space melted away until only the eternal flame remained, pure and infinite.

Just as quickly, the vision ended, gently returning Joren to himself. He drew a shuddering breath, blinking in awe at Antonius.

"By the gods...I never imagined..." Joren trailed off, words failing him.

Antonius clasped his shoulders, pride wreathing his face in smiles. "You did beautifully, young one. This was but the first spark - with training, you will harness the Phoenix's true power."

Joren returned the embrace fiercely, his heart overflowing with gratitude. There were no guarantees in the fight ahead, but this moment was a turning point. Whatever came, Joren knew with bone-deep certainty he would not face it alone. The eternal flame sheltered and strengthened all it touched.

Of that, he had never been more sure.

Chapter 16: Tidings of Doom

A pall of dread fell over Sadrym's winding halls as Antonius' grave summons rang out. Within minutes, the conservatory's highest-ranking mages gathered, their footsteps echoing anxiously through the marble corridors. Even the ancient oaks lining the pathways seemed to rustle and groan in foreboding.

When the last stragglers had trickled in, Antonius stood, his normally kind eyes dark with worry. "Friends, I have received dire news. Malazar has consumed the Oracle's heart."

Gasps and murmurs rippled through the assembly at this revelation. Joren went pale, bile rising in his throat. With the Oracle's immense power coursing through him, Malazar would be unstoppable.

"I fear this is not the extent of the tidings," Antonius continued heavily. "Malazar has also resurrected the Oracle's corpse as an undead slave. The fiend now commands it. The ultimate sacrilege. Something I did not think anyone was capable of. Even him..."

A shocked silence met his words. The Oracle had been a central deity across all lands, her wisdom and guidance protecting entire generations. To see her defiled so was soul-crushing.

Kolos was the first to find his voice. "Antonius...surely there is some hope still? Some way to defeat this evil?" Though he tried to hide it, desperation tinged his tone.

Antonius' eyes softened with empathy. Placing a bracing hand on Kolos' shoulder, the archmage responded gently, "There is always hope, son, so long as we stand united." Straightening, his expression grew resolute once more.

"Make no mistake, the days ahead will test us severely," Antonius cautioned. "But we are not yet lost. Hear me now - I propose we teleport the entirety of our school beyond Malazar's reach."

Whispers broke out at this suggestion. Teleporting even one person required intense magic. Transporting the massive conservatory complex was unheard of.

Antonius lifted a hand for silence before continuing. "In the mountains beyond the Elven realms, we may rebuild and regroup, devising a means to defeat Malazar." He turned his gaze to Joren. "There, we shall have time to unlock the full fire of the Phoenix."

Though hesitant murmurs still echoed, hope glimmered in the mages' eyes.

The plan was bold, but it was a chance. If Sadrym fell, all was lost.

In the wake of Antonius' pronouncement, preparations began immediately. Every mage lent their skills, weaving an elaborate teleportation matrix throughout the conservatory grounds. Students were swiftly evacuated through side portals to ensure their safety.

Soon, the normally vibrant gardens and halls stood eerily empty, stripped of their inhabitants. Only Joren's companions and the top sorcerers remained, making the final adjustments for the monumental spell.

As the last traces of magic were laid, a tense hush fell. All eyes turned to Antonius, awaiting his signal. The archmage inhaled deeply, drawing on his connection with Azyrion. Then, in a resonating tone, he began the incantation, ancient words of power echoing across the abandoned conservatory.

Immediately, the web of magic lit up, lines of shimmering symbols linking across buildings and courtyards. The air thrummed with gathering power as Antonius led the chant, the other mages adding their voices.

Joren watched in awe as the ritual crescendoed, the entire world seeming to vibrate and blur.

But it was short-lived. Without warning, the clear skies turned bruise-black, unnatural storms swirling violently above them.

Antonius' face became grave once more.

Chapter 17: The Unexpected Onslaught

An uncanny stillness hung over Sadrym as final preparations were underway for the realm-wide teleportation spell. But the silence was shattered when warning bells began pealing urgently from the watchtowers. Scouts had sighted Malazar's forces massing just over the horizon - the attack had come early.

Chaos erupted as Antonius swiftly issued commands, his voice magically amplified to carry throughout the conservatory. "Bar the gates! Divert all magic to shields and defenses!"

As sorcerers rushed to obey, Joren turned to Antonius, shock etched on his face. "How did Malazar know of our plans?"

The archmage's expression was grave. "It seems absorbing the Oracle has granted him dominion over space and time. He intends to strike before we slip beyond his grasp."

Before Joren could respond, reality itself seemed to fracture. Unnatural violet rifts tore through the very air, disgorging hordes of shambling corpses and skeletal beasts. Leading the nightmarish army was the Oracle's reanimated husk, now a massive rotting dracolich.

"It cannot be!" Antonius cried. "Even with the Oracle's power, casting portals should not be possible!"

From somewhere beyond the veil, Malazar's disembodied voice echoed, dripping with contempt. "You are an ignorant fool, Antonius. Nothing is beyond my reach now!" To emphasize his point, more spatial rifts yawned open, reinforcements pouring endlessly onto Sadrym's besieged grounds.

Antonius' face hardened with resolve. Turning to Kolos and the Paragons, he commanded, "Keep weaving the teleportation spell, no matter the cost! We must escape!"

As the mages redoubled their efforts, Antonius addressed the others. "Defend this place, my friends! We need but a little more time!" With that, the archmage strode forth to intercept the dracolich Oracle himself.

Joren, Lyra, Anwar and Rafaela swiftly joined the scores of students and teachers preparing to make a valiant last stand. They manned the parapets and barricades, weapons and spells primed to meet the coming onslaught.

When the first wave of undead broke against Sadrym's defenses, the battle was joined in earnest. The conservatory shone with magical light as its inhabitants unleashed their full might. Joren inhaled deeply, drawing on the Phoenix's nascent flame within. Fists wreathed in fire, he became a blur of punishing blows, incinerating corpses to ash.

Nearby, Lyra danced and wove between foes, her twin daggers dealing death with each calculated strike. Each time she vanished in an obscuring puff of smoke, more enemies fell, throats slit or poisoned blades buried in their undead flesh.

At the front gates, Anwar was a bulwark, his blessed sword and shield keeping the horde at bay. Though pressured from all sides, the paladin held fast, his teeth gritted in ferocious defiance. Rafaela channeled restorative energies through him, ensuring the gates held.

But despite the defenders' efforts, the undead pushed inexorably forward, driven by Malazar's dark will. For each one felled, more emerged from the spreading spatial rents. It was a war of attrition, one they could not hope to win.

Joren fought on anyway, consumed by determination to buy Kolos and the other casters enough time. But as he incinerated yet another advancing horror, cold despair gripped him. It would not be enough. They were going to fail.

In the distance, the titanic forms of Antonius and the Oracle could be seen battling atop Sadrym's highest tower. Even Antonius' mastery over the storm proved unable to counter the undead colossus for long. As its claws raked his flesh, the archmage fell to his knees.

With their leader defeated, the will to fight began hemorrhaging from Joren and the other defenders. They were out of time. As Malazar's laughter echoed mockingly around them, the rippling spatial gates disgorged a fresh tidal wave of monsters for the final assault.

Joren planted his feet, ready to die fighting to the last. But before the end came, the air was pierced by a ferocious screech - the fierce cry of a fox, reverberating with ancient power. A blinding flash split the heavens, leaving a massive lighting fox spirit hovering protectively over Sadrym.

"Behold Azyrion's true form!" Antonius' voice rang out, magically amplified once more. "We shall weather this storm together, brave defenders!"

Joren's heart swelled with renewed hope at the sight of the Storm Fox. Perhaps they yet had a chance if the founders' essences walked the earth again. With blazing fists raised high, Joren roared a defiant battle cry. As one, the defenders of Sadrym surged forth, determined to make their last stand a worthy one.

And so, beneath the spirit of a legendary guardian, the battle raged on, tilting dangerously on a knife's edge. Both sides knew this was the climax, with the very fate of the realm at stake. Joren only prayed when the dust settled, there would still be a future left to fight for.

As Azyrion's spectral fox form clashed violently with the corrupted Oracle above, Antonius descended from the parapets, his expression grimly determined. The archmage swiftly made his way to the inner sanctum where the teleportation spell was being feverishly woven.

Kolos looked up from the swirling magics, hope and dread both reflected in his eyes. "Master Antonius! What are your orders?"

Placing a bracing hand on his pupil's shoulder, Antonius said solemnly, "My place is no longer here, but on the front lines. I will buy you more time."

"But Master..." Kolos began pleadingly.

Antonius gently stopped him with a raised hand. "You know what must be done, Kolos. If we are to have any future, the spell must succeed." His gaze softened. "I have faith in you, son."

With a final comforting squeeze of Kolos' shoulder, Antonius strode towards the inner gates which still held against the undead siege. As they grinded open before him, the archmage turned back once more.

"No matter what transpires beyond these walls, do not falter. Lead them all to safety." Antonius' voice rang with conviction, the request both an order and a deeply personal entreaty.

Kolos mutely nodded, words failing him. With a sad smile, Antonius lifted his staff and walked through the gates to confront Malazar alone. They slowly boomed shut behind him, leaving Kolos surrounded by frantically casting mages.

Outside, Antonius' sudden presence sparked cries of dismay from the defending students. "Go back, Master! Save yourself!" they pleaded. But the archmage ignored them, striding forth until he stood atop a mound overlooking the teeming undead army.

Channeling magic through his staff, Antonius magnified his voice with a resounding crack. "Malazar! Face me, coward! End this invasion and let us settle matters without further innocent bloodshed!"

The battle seemed to still at Antonius' bold challenge. For several agonizing heartbeats, only silence answered. Then, with contemptuous laughter, Malazar materialized before the archmage in a haze of violet smoke.

"You wish to die so eagerly, old man?" the necromancer sneered. "I would be happy to grant your wish."

Antonius stood unfazed, his hawk-like gaze boring calmly into Malazar's baleful eyes. "If my life is the price for their safety, I pay it gladly," he intoned.

Malazar's lip curled, his spindly fingers tightening on his corrupted staff. "Your pathetic nobility sickens me. I will choke the life from you myself!"

As he took a threatening step forward, one of his Harpy lieutenants dove towards Antonius, its talons poised to shred the archmage's unprotected back. But quicker than blinking, Malazar lashed out with a whip of dark energy, wrapping it around the Harpy's throat.

"Do not meddle, worm!" he snarled, flexing his power to snap the Harpy's neck instantly. Tossing the limp corpse aside, Malazar refocused his malignant glare on Antonius.

"The old fool is mine," he hissed. "Stand ready, cur. I will grant you the mercy of a swift end." With gathering power, Malazar prepared a lethal curse upon his staff, murderous intent etched on his face.

~

Sparks flew as Antonius' and Malazar's staves collided in a dazzling display of arcane might. The very air hummed with gathering power as the two masters of magic clashed.

Antonius moved with the grace and ferocity he was famous for, raining potent lightning strikes upon his foe. But Malazar countered with sinister shadows, devouring each flash of light.

"Your tricks are feeble, old man," the necromancer taunted, serpentine ropes of darkness lashing from the Deathreaver Scepter.

Antonius deflected them with a shimmering shield. "The light always prevails, fiend," he intoned. With a sweeping gesture, he summoned gusting winds to batter his opponent.

Malazar only laughed. With necromantic sorcery, he drew strength from the newly dead corpses littering the battlefield. "You delay the inevitable."

The clash intensified, each unleashing their full arsenal. Antonius shone with beneficent magic, striking with the brilliance of a thousand suns. But Malazar corrupted all he touched, a vortex of despair.

As the duel raged, the conservatory's defenses groaned under the relentless assault of Malazar's forces. Without Antonius' direct support, the shields began to buckle.

Inside the sanctum, Kolos raced to reinforce the enchantments, even as he led the teleportation ritual. Sweat beaded his brow from the exertion as chaos escalated outside.

"The shields are collapsing!" someone cried. All around, mages braced themselves as the protective barriers ruptured completely with an earth-shattering blast.

Undead horrors flooded the breach, converging on the spell-chamber. Kolos' mind raced - there was no time left. Their only hope was the teleportation ritual. He shouted the final words of activation, magic exploding outward in a blinding nova.

Outside, the shockwave of energy briefly staggered both Antonius and Malazar. In that moment of distraction, the necromancer seized his opportunity.

With serpentine speed, Malazar invoked a deadly necrosis curse, noxious violet energy erupting from his staff towards Antonius' unprotected flank. At the last instant, the archmage sensed the attack and evoked a prismatic barrier, deflecting the brunt of the sorcery.

"Your malice will not sway me, monster," Antonius thundered. Sweeping his staff skyward, he summoned crackling meteors of pure cosmic energy, raining them down upon his foe with righteous fury.

Malazar screamed in agony as the meteors pummeled him, scorching his flesh. But he drew power from the darkness, healing his wounds. With a guttural chant, he ripped open a void rift, from which spilled a nightmarish horde of abyssal horrors.

"I will exterminate your light!" the necromancer vowed.

Unfazed, Antonius slammed his staff down, calling on the brilliance of the sun itself. Blinding solar flames ignited the creatures, burning them to cinders.

The epic duel raged on, Antonius' arcane power clashing against Malazar's desecration. Each sought to gain the upper hand, the very fate of the realm hanging in the balance.

Meanwhile, inside the conservatory's breached walls, chaos reigned. As Kolos desperately led the teleportation ritual, Professor Silvia engaged a hulking level 97 Undertaker in direct combat.

The elderly conjurer was deceptively agile, evading the undead brute's massive axe as she bombarded it with prismatic rays. Students and teachers assisted her assault, empowering her spells from afar while fending off encroaching corpses.

Step by bloody step, they kept the hordes from overwhelming Kolos and the teleportation mages. Outside, the final outcome rested on Antonius' duel. But their faith in the archmage remained unbroken. Until the last, they would stand together, Kindle's light against Malevolence's shadow.

Chapter 18: The Battle Within

Chaos engulfed the conservatory as Malazar's forces swarmed the breached gates. Joren slashed violently through the oncoming tide, determination etched on his face. In the distance, he could see Antonius' duel with Malazar intensifying, deadly magic exploding in dazzling displays.

Joren's heart pounded. He had to help Antonius! The archmage was one of the few wizards powerful enough to potentially stop Malazar for good. Gripped by urgency, Joren carved an opening and made for the gates.

But suddenly Antonius holographically projected himself there, blocking his path. The archmage's voice boomed, magically amplified. "Turn back, Joren! Your place is inside protecting the spell!"

Joren skidded to a halt, frustration boiling inside him. "But you need help!" he pleaded desperately. "I can't let you face him alone!"

Antonius' eyes softened. His essence placing a hand on Joren's shoulder, he responded gently, "My fate is chosen, dear boy. But yours still awaits. Guard this place so there is a future left to fight for."

"Go now!"

With that, Antonius turned back towards Malazar, not waiting for a response. Joren could only watch helplessly as the archmage strode away, silver robes billowing. He wanted to call out, to follow, but Antonius' words rooted him in place. Clenching his fists, Joren turned back to the spell-chamber.

The following hours were a blur of claws, fangs and steel. Corpses fell before Joren in droves, but their numbers barely dwindled. The undead had them completely overwhelmed, the defensive line collapsing bit by bit.

Joren roared in frustration, phoenix fire erupting in wild, uncontrolled bursts from his hands. But the spirit's full potential remained frustratingly sealed. Never had he felt so powerless.

As the night dragged on, exhaustion gradually took its toll. Nearby, Anwar was badly wounded, Rafaela desperately working to heal him. Even Kolos' magic faltered as he tried single-handedly sustaining the remaining enchantments.

Their eyes, brimming with hope and fear, turned to Joren. In past battles, he had always found a way to turn the tide. But this time, the Phoenix's voice was silent.

Doubt and anger clawed at Joren's mind. What was the point of harboring this so-called gift when he couldn't unlock its potential at their most dire hour?

Sensing his turmoil, Lyra placed a gentle hand on his shoulder. "Breathe," she urged. "Don't lose faith now. We'll find a way."

Her voice anchored him, soothing the maelstrom somewhat. She was right. Giving in to despair would only hasten their defeat. Their only course was to keep fighting.

Hours more dragged by in a haze of sweat, blood and mounting despair. Any scrap of ground gained was lost twice as fast. But amazingly, the defenders kept rising again, determined to buy every last second possible.

Finally, the inevitable happened. With an earth-shattering explosion, the last gate blew apart, undead flooding the inner sanctum. Before Joren knew it, the spell-weavers were surrounded. Through the chaos, his eyes locked with Lyra's. Then, moving as one, they leapt to intercept the tide.

Chapter 19: The Eternal Flame

With a guttural cry, Joren unleashed the Phoenix's elemental fury, decimating the undead hordes. But the tidal wave of power swiftly receded, dropping him limply to the ground as darkness claimed him.

Dread gripped Lyra's heart. "Joren!" She rushed to his side, cradling his limp form. To her relief, he still breathed, lost only to unconsciousness. The Phoenix's awakening had sapped his vitality entirely.

As Rafaela hurried to revive him, Joren's spirit drifted into the etheric plain, a realm beyond the physical. He found himself walking through tranquil waters, each step sending out gentle ripples across the glassy surface.

In the distance, upon a glowing dais, lay the magnificent form of an enormous phoenix wreathed in gentle flames. Though asleep, its power thrummed through the etheric realm. Joren's soul resonated in response as he drew nearer.

Kneeling reverently, Joren called out, "Great Phoenix, I have traveled far in search of you." His voice echoed strangely in the empty vastness.

At the sound, one of the Phoenix's glowing eyes partially opened. When it spoke, its voice was the crackling of an inferno. "I have watched you from within, child. Waiting until you were ready."

Joren's brows furrowed. "Ready? I have struggled long to awaken the fire within me. Why have you remained silent?" There was no accusation, only earnestness.

Fenria regarded him solemnly. "Power alone does not make one worthy. You still had much to learn about yourself, and your true purpose."

Chastened, Joren bowed his head. "Then help me understand, ancient one. Share with me your wisdom, so I may unlock the potential you granted me."

With ancient patience, Fenria explained. "The fire you seek burns in all mortal souls, though many do not feel its warmth. It is the flame of hope, of compassion, of life itself."

Her piercing eyes burned into Joren's. "Open your heart, child, and it will kindle the inferno within you. But never forget - you are the master, not the flame. It is but light to guide your way."

Joren mulled her words. In his desperation, he had come to regard the Phoenix's gift as a means to an end, a weapon to wield. But it was far greater than that. It was life. And it already flowed through him and those he cherished, through every soul that dreamt and hoped.

"I understand," he whispered thickly. "Thank you, Fenria, for this wisdom. I will walk in your light, and carry it for others."

Fenria inclined her splendid head. "Then go with my blessing, young spark. Dawn's first light approaches. The rest lies in your hands."

Her glowing eyes began to close once more as Joren's spirit drifted back towards his physical form. But before slumber claimed the phoenix, her voice echoed across the etheric plain one last time.

"Trust in those who love you. The greatest inferno arises from the kindling of shared hearts."

With a soft gasp, Joren awoke, his vision swimming into focus on Lyra's concerned face hovering anxiously over him. Beyond her, he could see the first golden rays of dawn breaking over the devastated conservatory. The light's warmth seemed to resonate through his very soul, rekindling faded embers.

Lyra exhaled in profound relief, drawing Joren into a fierce embrace. Over her shoulder, Joren's gaze met Kolos and the others, conveying wordless thanks and love. Together, they turned towards the dawn, hope dawning anew.

Chaos engulfed Sadrym as the casters channeled every shred of power into the teleportation ritual, their final desperate gambit. But maintaining the volatile spell matrix grew more difficult by the minute as Malazar's assault intensified.

Stone exploded in sprays of deadly shrapnel as undead horrors overran the outer courtyards, sieging the spell chamber itself. The surviving defenders formed a barricade of the rubble, struggling to buy the ritual more time.

Inside, the weeks of preparation were barely holding the unstable portal magics in check. As the school shook with the force of undead battering rams, cracks spread across the chamber dome like fracturing ice. They were out of time.

"Keep casting!" Kolos yelled hoarsely. "We cannot falter!" The mages redoubled their efforts, voices raised in strained unison, the final incantations reverberating through the collapsing halls.

The teleportation ritual teetered on the brink of collapse as the mages neared complete depletion. Incanting weakly, their life force drained by the unstable portal magics, despair crept over them. It wasn't enough.

Suddenly, Joren burst into the spell chamber, eyes blazing with amber light as the Phoenix spirit stirred within. Without hesitation, he joined their casting circle, exhaling deeply as he opened himself as a conduit.

The mages gasped as elemental fire flowed from Joren into the flickering portal matrix, bolstering the faltering magics. Energized by the phoenix essence, the ritual began stabilizing, the teleportation's activation imminent.

But channeling the Phoenix's ancient power came at a devastating cost.

Blood trickled from Joren's eyes and nose. He knew he couldn't keep this up for much longer. Such raw primal fire was not meant for mortal flesh.

Chapter 20: The Great Archmage

In the midst of the decaying battlefield outside of the Arcane Conservatory, a duel was unfolding between two of the most formidable powers in the realm. Antonius, the seasoned Archmage, and Malazar, the corrupted necromancer, clashed in a spectacular display of arcane power, each blow illuminating the eerie darkness that had befallen the ancient grounds.

Antonius, even in his twilight years, held his ground against the relentless onslaught of Malazar. Their spells danced in the air, weaving intricate patterns as they clashed and recoiled, creating dazzling arcs of elemental magic that scarred the very earth beneath their feet.

Despite the mounting fatigue, Antonius remained steadfast. His eyes, once filled with the warmth of knowledge and wisdom, now flickered with a sense of determination that belied his age. Each defensive barrier he cast, each retaliatory strike, bought him a few precious moments, moments he desperately needed for the complex teleportation spell to take effect.

Meanwhile, Malazar, his figure grotesque and menacing under the ominous, moonlit sky, unleashed a relentless barrage of necrotic energy. His eyes, lifeless and cold, glowed with an unholy light, the embodiment of his unfettered power and unbridled hatred.

"Your feeble attempts at defense are futile, Antonius!" he bellowed, his voice echoing through the desolate ruins. "Accept your fate and perish!"

"Never, Malazar," Antonius retorted, his voice unwavering. "I will not let your corruption taint these sacred grounds any further."

Their verbal exchange was but a minor distraction amidst the chaos of their magical duel. But as the minutes turned to hours, even Antonius's resolve began to falter. With each spell, each magical shield he conjured, his strength waned, his movements slowed, and his defenses faltered. He was growing weary, and Malazar was quick to take advantage.

In a final, desperate attack, Malazar hurled a concentrated ball of necrotic energy towards Antonius. Despite his efforts to dodge the onslaught, the spell hit Antonius square in the chest, the impact catapulting him back and sending him crashing to the ground.

As Antonius lay there, pain wracking his aged body, he noticed something through his blurred vision. The Arcane Conservatory, once standing tall and proud, had vanished. His last-ditch effort, the teleportation spell, had worked. A wave of relief washed over him, even as the world around him began to fade into obscurity, knowing his precious students, his beloved Conservatory and the heroes of a new age would be safe. At least for now.

Through his rapidly dimming vision, he could see the looming figure of Malazar approaching. The sneer on the necromancer's face was the last thing Antonius saw before his world plunged into darkness.

Chapter 21: An Unfamiliar Place

The chaos of their confrontation with Malazar had come to a chilling climax. As Joren channeled the potent life energy of the Phoenix into the intricate runes etched around the Arcane Conservatory, the hallowed grounds began to shimmer with ethereal light. The final strokes of the teleportation spell were being painted with fire and fury, birthing a spectral phoenix from the ashes of despair. As the spell completed, the world around them warped and twisted, fading into a cascade of shimmering lights, swallowing them whole into an in-between realm.

Their last memories were of a ground trembling beneath their feet, and a sky bending around them before everything went dark. Collapsed from the sheer force of the spell, they all succumbed to a restless slumber, suspended between reality and the echoes of arcane forces.

When Joren awoke, he was greeted by a world alien to him. A sprawling landscape of towering trees with leaves shimmering in hues of silver and gold. They were in an enchanted forest, untouched by the ravages of war and time.

Stumbling to his feet, Joren looked around. His friends, Rafaela, Kolos,

Lyra, and Anwar, lay strewn around him, just stirring from their forced slumber. The other mages who had been part of the Conservatory's last stand were slowly coming to terms with their new surroundings, their faces mirroring his confusion and relief.

"The teleportation spell...it worked," Rafaela whispered, her voice strained yet filled with wonder.

"But at what cost?" Lyra interjected, her gaze hardening as she glanced around at their unfamiliar surroundings.

"The cost was worth it, Lyra," Anwar's voice was stern, the weight of their escape pressing heavily on him, "We live to fight another day."

They found themselves in a sea of uncertainty. Yet, they were safe, alive, and that was all that mattered at that moment. Questions regarding Antonius's fate and the threat of Malazar hung in the air like a thick fog, casting long shadows over their brief respite.

Anwar's words seemed to anchor them all, drawing their focus back to their shared purpose. "We continue on, for Antonius, for the Conservatory, for all that is good in this world."

Joren nodded in agreement, his gaze falling on his hands, now drained of his fiery energy. The uncertainty of the future bore down upon him, yet within him, the flame of hope flickered, fueled by their resolve to face whatever trials lay ahead.

But even amidst the relief and determination, a cold dread slowly crept in. An ominous sensation that sent chills down their spines. As they looked around, taking in their new surroundings, their eyes were drawn towards the edge of the forest, where the shadows seemed to deepen and form grotesque shapes.

An uneasy silence hung over the mountain refuge as the survivors of Sadrym tried to regain their bearings. Although temporarily out of Malazar's reach, the lingering thrill of fear remained.

As Joren helped erect temporary shelters, Lyra kept watch from a rocky precipice. Her keen eyes constantly scanned the exotic woods that unfolded below, stretching to the horizon. A flash of movement in the tree line suddenly caught her attention.

Lyra's blood turned to ice. For an instant, she spotted two malevolent pinpricks of crimson light peering out from the shadows. But when she glanced again, they had vanished as if never there.

Unease coiled in her gut as she hurried back to the others. "I thought I saw something out there, watching from the trees," Lyra reported grimly. "Two red eyes, then gone again."

Anwar frowned, hand drifting to the hilt of his blessed sword. "What manner of creature could it be?

Anything Natural to a forest?" Kolos, lost in thought, responded ominously. "Perhaps, but given recent events, I doubt it. We must be on guard."

Nearby, Professor Silvia gave a solemn nod. "You are right to be wary, Kolos," the venerable sorceress said. "These are the Twilight Woods, last bastion of the Elves against Malazar's darkness. But if he has breached their borders..." She left the rest unspoken.

Lyra felt the truth like a leaden weight. Glancing at Joren, she asked the terrifying question. "Could Malazar have found us already?" Around the fire, faces paled at the possibility.

Professor Silvia's expression remained grave. "Impossible to say. But he has likely deduced the general vicinity, if only by process of elimination. Nowhere else could have shielded Sadrym's magic."

"Nowhere except here," Rafaela whispered. Dread bloomed in her chest. Would they never find peace from that monster's predations?

Sensing their despair, Silvia softened her tone. "Do not abandon hope yet. The Elves are ancient and cunning. Their magicks hide this domain well. We may still have time."

Despite her reassurance, none felt comforted. Malazar's power seemed to corrupt all it touched, a cancer on the living world. How long could even the elves resist that creeping blight?

As the day waned, Joren found a quiet moment to meditate, reaching inward for the Phoenix's guidance. Its presence blazed brighter now within him, tempered by wisdom. But anticipation thrummed through their bond. The fated confrontation loomed nearer.

Fenria's whisper came as distant fire. "The shadow stirs, young spark. Will you shine against its hatred?"

Joren silently swore he would. But fear and doubt still plagued him. Was the flame within enough to banish the dark? Or would its light too fade to cold ash?

Sensing his anxiety, Fenria soothed him. "Darkness cannot smother a candle unless one concedes defeat. Remember this in the struggle ahead." With that cryptic remark, the Phoenix withdrew, leaving Joren to ponder alone as dusk deepened.

In the days that followed, an unsettling quiet took hold, broken only by reports of brief sightings of those hateful crimson eyes spying from the gloom. Each glimpse fueled dread that the jaws of the trap were inexorably closing.

Preparations progressed feverishly for the coming storm. But Joren noticed the mages casting worried glances to the shadows more frequently, their songs dying on nervous lips. Even ancient professor Silvia seemed perturbed, her spells of concealment faltering as resolve wavered.

But Joren clung fiercely to Fenria's words. Their light could not fail so long as anyone nurtured its flame. Even if shadow sought to smother the world, the spark endured so long as hope remained. In that conviction, Joren found courage.

On the sixth dusk since arriving, the pall of tension finally broke. As Joren helped erect a shelter, Gavros, the lead scout, came sprinting back through the woods, panic etched on his face. His horse had returned riderless.

The camp dissolved into frightened chaos at the realization. Their haven had been discovered. All knew ghastly foes now surged towards them, numbering in the thousands. Nowhere to run or hide remained. The light would be tested as never before.

Joren trembled but forced down his terror. Glancing at his dearest companions, he swore to stand by them, no matter how the darkness raged. If this were to be their end, they would fall united, the Phoenix's flame never extinguished.

There was still hope. Fenria's voice echoed once more, ethereal but clear. "Have courage, young spark. The echoes of twilight await."

The shadows lengthened and crimson eyes glittered just beyond the firelight. But Joren stood tall, his spirit kindled. Let them come. Light endured.

Epilogue

The Twilight Realm

Lore:

Beyond the Mortal tapestry, hidden in the shadows between worlds, lies the Twilight Realm. This timeless domain has been homeland to the Elves since primordial eras when gods still walked the earth.

As mortal civilizations rose and fell around them, the Elves remained isolated in their sanctuary, indifferent to fleeting mundane conflicts. Even the coming of Malazar barely stirred them from their apathetic stupor.

Only when refugees began intruding into their sacred forests did the Elves take notice, expelling the desperate mortals with callous indifference. Malazar and his corruption remained a distant concern barely worth acknowledging.

For centuries, the Twilight Realm endured untouched, its mystic beauty preserved in flawless stasis. Ancient creatures from legends roamed its woods and mountains, specters of a bygone age. The rivers ran silver with ancestral magic, nourishing trees that predated mortal reckoning.

But immortal perfection demanded isolation. So the Elves continued withdrawing, sealing their thriving lands away from the withering mortal plane. Only the most desperate fugitives might chance glimpsing that forgotten country, and few returned to tell of it.

To most, it passed into myth, a timeless echo of life unfettered by death or darkness. But oblivious in their paradise, the Elves took no notice.

Only with Malazar's power swelling, his hordes pressing against their magical barriers, did the Elves reluctantly take interest in the mortal plight. For if light failed utterly among men, darkness would inevitably encroach, corrupting the Twilight Realm's perfection.

This concern was not born of mercy. The Elves remained as ruthlessly pragmatic as they were beautiful. If mankind fell, so too would the balance holding Malazar's blight at bay. Such could not be tolerated.

But their seclusion had lasted eons. Rejoining a conflict long ignored did not come naturally, the plight of mere mortals beneath immortal notice. Yet, failure to act courted graver consequence.

It remained to be seen whether such flickers would suffice to ignite daybreak's first light. But with allies thought mythical emerging from legend's shadows, there yet remained a chance, however slim.

All that was certain was the dusk would be long and cruel. Much would be sacrificed before a new dawn's genesis could be fathomed. Standing vigilant against encroaching night demanded steely wills untainted by despair.

Darkness falls, but light endures in even the frailest ember, so long as the flame's keepers persist.

To Be Continued...

Thank you for reading.

To receive emails regarding upcoming book deals, free book giveaways and updates on release dates sign up at:

https://joelpoe.com/contact/

*Consider sharing your experience on **Amazon** and **Goodreads**. Reviews and ratings from readers like you help new readers find this book.*

Plus, it is what helps me measure your interest in this particular story, to decide whether I should write more sequels.

Till next time,

Joel Poe

Joel Poe

Printed in Great Britain
by Amazon